Rennell Rodd

Poems in Many Lands

Rennell Rodd

Poems in Many Lands

ISBN/EAN: 9783337207069

Printed in Europe, USA, Canada, Australia, Japan

Cover: Foto ©Andreas Hilbeck / pixelio.de

More available books at **www.hansebooks.com**

POEMS IN MANY LANDS

Ballantyne Press

BALLANTYNE, HANSON AND CO., EDINBURGH
CHANDOS STREET, LONDON

POEMS IN MANY LANDS

BY

RENNELL RODD

LONDON
DAVID BOGUE, 3, ST. MARTIN'S PLACE
TRAFALGAR SQUARE, W.C.
1883.

PREFACE.

THE kind reception my first small volume of " Songs in the South" met with, has induced me to include a few of those poems in this more complete volume of early lyrics.

I have to acknowledge the permission to reprint one or two poems which have been previously published in magazines, or as songs.

R. R.

December, 1882.

CONTENTS.

viii CONTENTS.

A STAR-DREAM.

THERE was a night when you and I
    Looked up from where we lay,
When we were children, and the sky
    Was not so far away.

We looked towards the deep dark blue
    Beyond our window bars,
And into all our dreaming drew
    The spirit of the stars.

We did not see the world asleep—
    We were already there !
We did not find the way so steep
    To climb that starry stair.

And faint at first and fitfully,
    Then sweet and shrill and near,
We heard the eternal harmony
    That only angels hear ;

B

And many a hue of many a gem
 We found for you to wear,
And many a shining diadem
 To bind about your hair.

We saw beneath us faint and far
 The little cloudlets strewn,
And I became a wandering star,
 And you became my moon.

Ah! have you found our starry skies?
 Where are you all the years?
Oh, moon of many memories!
 Oh, star of many tears!

THE DAISY.

WITH little white leaves in the grasses,
  Spread wide for the smile of the sun,
It waits till the daylight passes,
  And closes them one by one.

I have asked why it closed at even,
  And I know what it wished to say :
There are stars all night in the heaven,
  And I am the star of day.

"THOSE DAYS ARE LONG DEPARTED."

THOSE days are long departed,
 Gone where the dead dreams are,
Since we two children started
 To look for the morning star.

We asked our way of the swallow
 In his language that we knew,
We were sad we could not follow
 So swift the dark bird flew.

We set our wherry drifting
 Between the poplar trees,
And the banks of meadows shifting
 Were the shores of unknown seas.

We talked of the white snow prairies
 That lie by the Northern lights,
And of woodlands where the fairies
 Are seen in the moonlit nights.

Till one long day was over
   And we grew too tired to roam,
And through the corn and clover
   We slowly wandered home.

Ah child ! with love and laughter
   We had journeyed out so far ;
We who went in the big years after
   To look for another star ;

But I go unbefriended
   Through wind and rain and foam,—
One day was hardly ended
   When the angel took you home.

IN APRIL.

THE diamond dew lies cool
   In the violet cups athirst,
   The buds are ready to burst,
The heart of the spring is full ;
Great clouds dream over the sky,
   The drops on the grass-blades glisten,
   The daffodil droops to listen
As the wind from the South goes by,
For it came through the sea cliffs hollow,
   With the dawning over the bay,
And the swallow, it said, the swallow,
   The swallow comes home to-day.

IN THE WOODS.

THIS is a simple song
That the world sings every day,
Hark! as ye pass along
Ye that go by the way!
For the nightingale up in the oak-bough sings,
" *Be loyal, be true, true, true,*"
And the wood-dove sits with its folded wings,
And answers " *to you, to you.*"
And the thrush in the hedge, " *I am glad, be glad,*"
And the linnet, " *let love, let live,*"
·And the wind in the rushes says, " *why so sad !*"
And the wind in the trees " *forgive !*"
While ever so high in the skies above
The heart of the lark o'erflows,
And " *I love, I love, and I love,*"
Is the only song he knows.
Hark! as ye pass along
Ye that go by the way!
This is the simple song
That the world sings every day.

A SUMMER SONG.

SUMMER in the world and morning, the far hills were
    in the mist,
And we watched the river borders, how the rush and
    ripple kist,
While the bird sang " Whither, whither," and the
    wind said, " Where I list."

And we saw the yellow kingcup, and the arrowhead
    look through,
From the silent, shallow waters, where the mirrored
    skies were blue,
And the flags about the swan's nest kept the secret
    that we knew.

In the hedge a thrush was singing, where the wild
    hopclusters are,
And the lowly ragged-robin, with its fraily fretted
    star,
While a soft wind brought the fragrance of the
    meadow-sweet from far.

All its blushing bells a' ringing, on a bank the fox-
  glove grows,
Where the honeysuckle tangles in the thorns of the
  wild rose,
And a sudden sea of blue-bells from the wood-side
  overflows.

And we watched the silver crescent of the wings of
  the wild dove
Circle swiftly in the sunlight through the aspen tops
  above,
And we felt the great world's heart beat, in the gladness of our love.

THE BURDEN OF AUTUMN.

WE are dying, said the flowers,
    All the days are out of tune,
Spent are all the sungold hours,
    And the glory that was June,
Dying, dying said the flowers.
      The snow will hide the garden bed
        While they sleep underground,
      Wild winds will drift it overhead,
        But they will slumber sound.

We are going, said the swallows,
    All the singing days are done,
Summer's over, winter follows,
    And we seek a warmer sun,
Going southward, said the swallows.
      And I must watch them all depart
        And find no song to sing,
      Oh take the autumn from my heart
        And give me back the spring !

"TO WONDER AND BE STILL."

OFT in the starry middle night
    I vex my heart in vain,
To set its mystic music right,
    And find the hidden strain.

To-night the summer moon is strong,
    The little clouds drift past,—
The wonder is too deep for song—
    The silence speaks at last.

" Thou canst not match those harmonies
    On moon-enamoured lute,
Serenely silent arch the skies,
    And the great stars are mute ;

" Thou canst not tune to thine unrest
    Their solemn calm above ;
In silence thou shalt worship best,
    And reverently love.

" Beyond this night in which thou art,
    There is a voice of spheres,
Which the eternal in thine heart
    Remembers and reveres.

" But how they sing in unison
    Earth's ear hath never heard,
So only in thine heart rings on
    The song that has no word."

AN ANSWER.

TAKE again thy shallow hearted reason
    Groping dimly through the night in which thou
        art !
Very harmless fall the arrows of thy treason
    On the worship and the wonder in my heart.

I have drunk the everlasting fountains
    Flowing downward from the infinite to me,
Seen the wonder of the moonrise in the mountains
    And the glory of the sunset on the sea.

THE POET.

HE will come again as oft of old among you,
   With his burden to fulfil ;—
Did ye hearken ever to the songs they sung you
   Till the song was still ?

HE will bear again the scorn, the idle wonder,
   And heart-hunger and love's need ;
You will drown the sound of music in your thunder,
   And he will not heed.

Singing unperplexed above the mocking laughter
   Till his day be overpast ;
Till the music dies, and silence follows after
   And ye turn at last,—

Then when all the echoes breathe it and ye know it,
   Ye will seek him to revere ;
Cry aloud, and call him, master, lover, poet !
   And he will not hear.

VICTORY.

THIS then—to live and have no joy thereof,
To thirst and hunger and be very tired,
To walk unloved, or know if one should love
It were a bitter thing that he desired,
To have no home in all the earth, to be
Mocked and derided and outcast of men,
To squander love and labour, and to see
No fruit of it, and yet to love, and then
Bearing all slander silently alway,
Serenely when the last reproach is hurled
To look Death in the face alone, and say
"Be of good cheer for I have overcome the world."

"AH! WILD SWANS!"

"AH! wild swans winging southward, I would fly with
    you to-night;
Southward, ever swiftly southward, through the
    autumn grey twilight.

"You will leave these downs and gullies, and the white
    cliffs far behind,
Sailing on above the waters in the music of the
    wind.

"And the seamen on their highway looking up will
    see you fly,
Like a misty shadow moving o'er the moon-illumined
    sky.

"Day and night and all things changing,—sunny skies
    and overcast,—
Till the cloud-engirdled mountains and the snowy
    peaks are passed.

" We should near the lands of laughter and the vines
  and olive trees,
Watch the little sails at sundown sparkle out on
  summer seas ;

" Day and night and ever flying till we reached the
  wonderland,
And the seaward branching river, and the desert ways
  of sand ;

" Saw beneath us standing lonely that grave bird that
  never sings,
Like a solemn sentry guarding by the giant tombs
  of kings.

" And I think it would be sunset when our journeying
  was done,
And the silver of your plumage would be crimsoned
  in the sun ;

" In a pleasant land of palm-trees, where the lotus lilies
  grow,
And the fruits of many flood-tides by the river
  borders blow ;

C

" There forgetting and forgotten, and not any one to
  hear,
I would sing to you, that sing not, all the winter of
  the year."

Brighter burn the stars and colder, twilight deepens
  into night,
Moans the wind among the willows, and the swans
  fade out of sight.

DAY'S END.

WE watched how robed in royal red
  The slow sun sailed to rest,
Through crimson cloud streaks islandèd
  In seas of glory o'er the west,
I held your hand, and I heard you say,
"What have we done for the world to-day?"

While still the mountain-heather glowed
  All songs were hushed, and through
The twilight east the young moon showed
  Her frail white crescent in the blue ;
The silence sank profound and deep,
The ways of earth were full of sleep ;
And the spirit of silence seemed to say,
" What have ye done for the world to-day?"

FROM THE ROADSIDE.

PEACE be with the little red-roofed church out yonder,
  With its quiet English village gathered round ;
With shade of great beech-trees on the grave-mounds
    under,
  And leaves of the Autumn over all the ground!

There go the rooks at even homeward flying!
  The sweet sense of home lies over all that land ;
The glow is on the tower of the daylight dying,
  And lovers in the shadow are walking hand-in-
    hand.

Here comes no voice from the middle world to move
    them,
  All the year round no memorable thing ;
Yet the great skies arch as beautiful above them,
  All the year through there are birds with them
    that sing.

Ah! well with you who calm and little knowing,

    Here in submission to your uneventful days,

Leave the mad world to its coming and its going,

    Safe with God's shadow on your evening ways!

A DIRGE FOR LOVE.

"WHAT is this pitiful song ye sing,
    Shades of the passing hours ?
What is this beautiful young dead thing,
    Borne on a bier of flowers ?"

"This is dead Love who, all night through,
    Beat at the fast-closed door ;
Wept his heart out waiting for you,
    Now he will beat no more !

"Here he dwelt for a night and day,
    Longer he might not wait ;
Never again will he pass this way,
    Therefore we sing 'too late !'"

"Ah, but the door of my heart within,
    Was it not alway wide ?
Had he not wings to have entered in,
    Why did he beat outside ? "

" Once he came, though his eyes were blind,
　Up to the outer door ;
The way within was too hard to find,
　Peace ! For he wakes no more."

" Yet ye knew I had waited long,
　Was I not always true?
How could I will sweet Love this wrong—
　Where do ye bear him to ?"

" Back to the land where he lives again,
　Over the westward strand ;
Over the waves and the cloud domain,
　Into the rainbow land !"

" Then, sweet spirits, do this for grace,
　Set my heart on his bier ;
So, when he comes to his resting-place,
　Love may awake and hear !"

NOS COLLINES D'AUTREFOIS.

CAN you remember when we dwelt together,
In the golden land of childhood long ago ;
Up on our mountain heights in the clear weather,
How we longed to see the valleys down below ?

Lands so lovely never found we after,—
Oh, our winters with the wonder of their snows ;
Oh, the swallows of our spring-time, and the laughter,
Oh, the starnight of our summers and the rose !

Well-belovèd, in that land were all the faces,
None are like them of these dwellers in the plain ;
Oh, why did we come down from our high places !
We can never climb the bitter hills again !

THE TWO GATES.

Two gates—and one was morning's, gold with gleams
    Of sudden sunlight, and clear skies above
    Ways where the air is musical with love,
And summer singing in a land of streams :

One sad with twilight and low sound that seems
    Like the marred song-voice of a broken heart,
    Where life and love sit evermore apart,
And look back longing to the gate of dreams.

Time was, I wandered in those sunlit lands,
    And felt the glamour in my wakening eyes ;
But now with sword aflame the angel stands,
    Pointing the threshold of the gate of gloom ;
    While through the monotone of human cries,
    Upsoars this pitiless, " fulfil thy doom !"

GETTATI AL VENTO.

I.

THE sea swallows wheel and fly
  To their homes in the grey cliff-side ;
And the silent ships drift by,
  The world and its ways are wide !

Oh, which of you wandering sails
  Will carry a word from me ?
Spread all your wings in the gales,
  Fly fast to her northern sea !

Go say to my heart's desired,
  Too long from her side I roam,
And say I am tired, tired,
  And I would she would call me home !

II.

I thought that I wandered, wandered,
  All night till the dawn of day,
And I came to the house she dwells in,
  A hundred miles away :

So I watched the hills grow golden,
    I heard the birds begin,
And she came to open her window,
    And let the morning in.

But when she would not greet me,
    And I called to her all in vain,
I awoke, and knew I was dreaming,
    But I could not sleep again.

I.

WHAT shadow is this of dead delight,
    That thou art dreaming of?
Oh, heart, what ails thee in the evenlight,
    And is it thine old burden love,
That wistful-eyed, like one who roams,
    I stand and watch from far,
The peace of sunset over quiet homes,
    And the belovéd evening star?

II.

Are not the heavens wide?   And yet,
　　Until all journeyings be done,
No star shall change the orbit set,
　　That marks its journey round the sun.

And, sweet, we travel down our days,
　　As the stars wander in their sky ;
We cannot change our fated ways,
　　But meet and greet and hasten by.

III.

I breathed a name once and again,
I said a bitter thing in my pain,
"I gave you all my love, and I spent it all in
　　vain ! "

Then I saw a form across the night
Glide down the stars in a veil of light,
And I said, "Who are you, dweller of the Infinite ?"

And I heard a voice on the stilly air,
"You chide amiss in your own despair;
Lo, I am the soul of her love, and I follow you
　　everywhere ! "

THE SEA-KING'S GRAVE.

HIGH over the wild sea-border, on the furthest
    downs to the west,

Is the green grave-mound of the Norseman, with
    the yew-tree grove on its crest.

And I heard in the winds his story, as they leapt up
    salt from the wave,

And tore at the creaking branches that grow from
    the sea-king's grave.

Some son of the old-world Vikings, the wild sea-
    wandering lords,

Who sailed in a snake-prowed galley, with a terror
    of twenty swords.

From the fiords of the sunless winter, they came on
    an icy blast,

Till over the whole world's sea-board the shadow of
    Odin passed,

Till they sped to the inland waters and under the
    South-land skies,

And stared on the puny princes, with their blue
    victorious eyes.

And they said he was old and royal, and a warrior
    all his days,
But the king who had slain his brother lived yet
    in the island ways ;
And he came from a hundred battles, and died in
    his last wild quest,
For he said, "I will have my vengeance, and then
    I will take my rest."

He had passed on his homeward journey, and the
    king of the isles was dead ;
He had drunken the draught of triumph, and his
    cup was the Isle-king's head ;
And he spoke of the song and feasting, and the
    gladness of things to be,
And three days over the waters they rowed on a
    waveless sea ;
Till a small cloud rose to the shoreward, and a gust
    broke out of the cloud,
And the spray beat over the rowers, and the
    murmur of winds was loud
With the voice of the far-off thunders, till the
    shuddering air grew warm,
And the day was as dark as at even, and the wild
    god rode on the storm.

But the old man laughed in the thunder as he set
    his casque on his brow,

And he waved his sword in the lightning and clung
    to the painted prow.

And a shaft from the storm-god's quiver flashed out
    from the flame-flushed skies,

Rang down on his war-worn harness and gleamed
    in his fiery eyes,

And his mail and his crested helmet, and his hair,
    and his beard burned red ;

And they said, " It is Odin calls ;" and he fell, and
    they found him dead.

So here, in his war-guise armoured, they laid him
    down to his rest,

In his casque with the rein-deer antlers, and the long
    grey beard on his breast ;

His bier was the spoil of the islands, with a sail for
    a shroud beneath,

And an oar of his blood-red galley, and his battle-
    brand in the sheath ;

And they buried his bow beside him, and planted
    the grove of yew,

For the grave of a mighty archer, one tree for each
    of his crew ;

Where the flowerless cliffs are sheerest, where the
    sea-birds circle and swarm,
And the rocks are at war with the waters, with their
    jagged grey teeth in the storm ;
And the huge Atlantic billows sweep in, and the
    mists enclose
The hill with the grass-grown mound where the
    Norseman's yew-tree grows.

DISILLUSION.

AH ! what would youth be doing
　　To hoist his crimson sails,
To leave the wood-doves cooing,
　　The song of nightingales ;
To leave this woodland quiet
　　For murmuring winds at strife,
For waves that foam and riot
　　About the seas of life ?

From still bays, silver sanded,
　　Wild currents hasten down
To rocks where ships are stranded
　　And eddies where men drown.
Far out, by hills surrounded,
　　Is the golden haven gate,
And all beyond unbounded
　　Are shoreless seas of fate.

They steer for those far highlands
　　Across the summer tide

D

And dream of fairy islands
    Upon the further side.
They only see the sunlight,
    The flashing of gold bars ;
But the other side is moonlight
    And glimmer of pale stars.

They will not heed the warning
    Blown back on every wind,
For hope is born with morning,
    The secret is behind.
Whirled through in wild confusion,
    They pass the narrow strait,
To the sea of disillusion
    That lies beyond the gate.

ON THE BORDER HILLS.

So the dark shadows deepen in the trees
    That crown the border mountains, all the air
Is filled with mist-begotten phantasies
    Shaped and transfigured in the sunset glare.
What wildly spurring warrior-wraiths are these?
    What tossing headgear, and what red-gold hair?
What lances flashing, what far trumpet's blare,
    That dies along the desultory breeze?

Slow night comes creeping with her misty wings
    Up to the hill's crest, where the yew trees grow;
About their shadow-haunted circle clings
    The rumour of an unrecorded woe,
Old as the battle of those border kings
    Slain in the darkling hollow-lands below.

WHEN HE HAD FINISHED.

WHEN He had finished, first his orbèd sun
Blazed through the startled firmament, and all
His hosts cried glory, and the stars each one
Sang joy together,—then did there not fall
A peace of solemn silence on His world,
A moment's hush before one leaf was stirred
Or one wave o'er the ocean mirror curled !
Lo ! then it was the carol of a bird
Gave the joy-note of being, up the sky
Some lark's song mounted and the young greenwood
Woke to a matin of wild melody,—
And He looked down and saw that it was good.

THE LONELY BAY.

HOLLOWED and worn by tide on tide
The rocks are steep, to the water's side ;
Never a swimmer might hope to land
With the sheer, sheer rocks upon either hand ;
Never a ship dare enter in
For the sunken reefs are cruel and thin ;
Only at times a plaintive moan
Comes from yon arch in the caverned stone,
When the seals that dwell in the ocean cave
Rise to look through the lifting wave ;
Only the gulls as they float or fly
Answer the waves with their wind-borne cry.

Weeds of the waste uptossed lie there
On the sandy space that the tide leaves bare,
Ever at ebb some waif or stray
That ever the flood wave washes away,
And round and round in the lonely bay.

And one dwells there in the caves below
That only the seals and the seagulls know,
And the haunting spirit is passing fair
With sea-flowers set in her grey-green hair,
But she looks not oft to the daylight skies
For the sunshine dazzles her ocean eyes ;
But now and again the sea-winds say,
In the twilight hour of after-day,
They have seen her look through her veil of spray.

Stilled are the waves when she lies asleep
And the stars are mirrored along the deep,
The gulls are at rest on the rifted rocks
And slumbering round are the ocean flocks,
Where the waving oarweeds lull and lull
And the calm of the water is beautiful.

But ever and aye in the moonless night,
When the waves are at war and the surf is white,
When the storm-wind howls in the dreary sky,
And the storm-clouds break as it whirls them by ;
When it tears the boughs from the churchyard tree
And they think in the world of the folk at sea,
When the great cliffs quake in the thunder's crash

And the gulls are scared at the lightning flash,
You will hear her laugh in the depths below,
Where the moving swell is a sheet of snow,
Mocking the mariner's shriek of woe.

Let us away, for the sky grows wild
And the wind has the voice of a moaning child !
And if she looked through her veil of spray,
And called and beckoned, you might not stay ;
You would leap from the height to her cold embrace
And drown in the smile of her wanton face !
She would carry you under the mazy waves
From deep to deep of her ocean caves,
Hold you fast with the things that be
Held in the drifts of the drifting sea,
Round and round for eternity !
The sun goes under, away, away !
It's dark and weird by the lonely bay.

MUSIC.

WHAT angel viol, effortless and sure,
    Speaks through the straining silence, whence, ah
        whence
That tremulous low joy, so keen, so pure
    That all existence narrows to one sense,
            Lapped round and round
            In rapture of sweet sound ?
Oh, how it wins along the steep, and loud and loud,
    Over the chasm and the cloud,
        Swells in its lordly tide
Higher and higher, and undenied,
        Full throated to the star !—
Then lowlier, softer, dreaming dies and dies
        Over the closing eyes,
    Dies with my spirit away, afar,
        Swayed as on ocean's breast
        Dies into rest.

"WHAT HOLDS THEE BACK?"

WHAT holds thee back then ? Hast thou aught to do,
And fearest for the venture, art thou too,
So light a thing that every wind blows through ?

What hast thou envied in the lives of these,
That thou should'st heed to please them or displease
And fill thine own with mirrored mockeries ?

This arm of thine is thine alone, and strong
To thy free service through thy whole life long,
Hear thine heart's voice, it will not lead thee wrong !

WORDS FOR MUSIC.

I.

THE autumn wind goes sighing
    Through the quivering aspen tree,
The swallows will be flying
    Toward their summer sea ;
The grapes begin to sweeten
    On the trellised vine above,
And on my brows have beaten
    The little wings of love.
Oh wind if you should meet her
    You will whisper all I sing !
Oh swallow fly to greet her,
    And bring me word in spring !

II.

I SEE your white arms gliding,
    In music o'er the keys,
Long drooping lashes hiding
    A blue like summer seas:

The sweet lips wide asunder,
   That tremble as you sing,
I could not choose but wonder,
   You seemed so fair a thing.

For all these long years after
   The dream has never died,
I still can hear your laughter,
   Still see you at my side ;
One lily hiding under
   The waves of golden hair ;
I could not choose but wonder,
   You were so strangely fair.

I keep the flower you braided
   Among those waves of gold,
The leaves are sere and faded,
   And like our love grown old.
Our lives have lain asunder,
   The years are long, and yet,
I could not choose but wonder,
   I cannot quite forget.

III.

ALL through the golden weather
    Until the autumn fell,
Our lives went by together
    So wildly and so well.——

But autumn's wind uncloses
    The heart of all your flowers,
I think as with the roses,
    So hath it been with ours.

Like some divided river
    Your ways and mine will be,
——To drift apart for ever,
    For ever till the sea.

And yet for one word spoken,
    One whisper of regret,
The dream had not been broken
    And love were with us yet.

IV.

I REMEMBER low on the water
    They hung from the dripping moss,
In the broken shrine of some streamgod's daughter
    Where the north and south roads cross ;
    And I plucked some sprays for my love to wear,
    Some tangled sprays of maidenhair.

So you went north with the swallow
    Away from this southern shore,
And the summers pass, and the winters follow,
    And the years, but you come no more,
    You have roses now in your breast to wear,
    And you have forgotten the maidenhair.

And the sound of the echoing laughter,
    The songs that we used to sing,
To remember these in the years long after
    May seem but a foolish thing,—
    Yet I know to me they are always fair
    My withered sprays of maidenhair.

V.

THE wide seas lay before us
  The moon was late to rise,
The skies were starry o'er us
  And Love was in our eyes ;
And " like those stars, abiding,"
  You whispered " Love shall be,"
Then one great star went gliding
  Right down into the sea.

Since then beyond recalling
  How many moons have set !
And still the stars keep falling,
  But the sky is starry yet :
And I look up and wonder
  If they can hear and know,
For still we walk asunder,
  And that was years ago.

BELLA DONNA.

Two tear-drops of the bluest seas
    Were prisoned in those laughing eyes,
And soft as wind in summer trees
    The music of her low replies ;
A sunbeam caught entangled there
Makes light in all her golden hair ;

The wild rose where the wild bees sip
    Is not so delicate as this,
And yet that little rose-curled lip
    Is very poisonous to kiss,
And they were stars of wintry skies
That lit the lustre in her eyes.

And she will smile and bid you stay
    And love a little at her will,
And love a little—and betray
    But smile as ever sweetly still ;
She knows that roses fade away,
    To-morrows turn to yesterday.

She walks the smooth and easy ways
  Apparelled in her queenly dress,
She hears no word that is not praise,
  And ever of her loveliness ;
And she will kill, that cannot hate,
  Dispassionately passionate.

JOSEPH BARA.

IN the year of battles, ninety-three,
In Vendée, by the westward sea,
The word was whispered—*Liberty.*

There was a child that would not stay,
When he watched them arm and ride away,
For the sword was bared in la Vendée.

Thirteen years, and girl-like fair,
With blue wide eyes and yellow hair—
And the word had moved him unaware.

"Mother," he said, "if I were old,
My arm should win the young ones gold—
A boy's life may be dearly sold.

E

" Mother, the hearts of the children bleed,
There are lips enough for one hand to feed,
And the youngest born have the greater need."

In the year of battles, ninety-three,
In Vendée by the westward sea,
He rode to fight for liberty.

They wondered how his stedfast eye
Could see the strong men bleed and die,
His shrill lips shape the battle cry.

At Chollet, in the month Frimaire
They found the lion in his lair,
And long the struggle wavered there.

Till wide and scattered, man with man,
The bloody waves of battle ran,
The boy was leading in the van.

His bugle at his waist he wore,
His sword-arm pointing straight before,
And on his brow the tricolore.

Horse and rider overthrown,
Lay about him stark as stone,
The bugle boy stood all alone.

They closed about him menacing,
To strike him seemed a murderous thing ;
"Take life, cry homage to the King !"

Fearless their bayonets he eyed,
The dead he loved were at his side,
And " Vive la République," he cried.

Sword thrust and bayonet
In his young heart's-blood met,
The groan died in his lips hard set,
And through his eyes shone life's regret.

O'er his torn and bleeding breast
All the storm of battle pressed,—
He lay lowly with the rest.

When the bitter fight was done
There they found their little one,
Stark and staring at the sun.

Freedom, let thy banners wave,
Where he lies among the brave,
For that young fresh life he gave!

Song above the names that die
Shrine his name in memory!

IN CHARTRES CATHEDRAL.

THROUGH yonder windows stained and old,
Four level rays of red and gold
    Strike down the twilight dim,
Four lifted heads are aureoled
    Of the sculptured cherubim,
And soft like sounds on faint winds blown
    Of voices dying far away,
The organ's dreamy undertone,
    The murmur while they pray ;
And I sit here alone, alone,
    And have no word to say ;
Cling closer shadows, darker yet,
    And heart be happy to forget.

And now, the mystic silence—and they kneel,
    A young priest lifts a star of gold,—
And then the sudden organ peal !
    Ave and Ave ! and the music rolled
Along the carven wonder of the choir,
Thrilled canopy and spire,

Up till the echoes mingled with the song ;
   And now a boy's flute note that rings
Shrill sweet and long,
   Ave and Ave, louder and more loud,
Rises the strain he sings,
   Upon the angel's wings !
   Right up to God !

And you that sit there in the lowliest place,
   With lips that hardly dare to move;
You with the old sad furrowed face,
   Dream on your dream of love !
For you, glide down the music's swell
   The folding arms of peace,
For me wild thoughts, I dare not tell
   Desires that never cease.
For you the calm, the angel's breast,
   Whose dim foreknowledge is at rest ;
For me the beat of broken wings,
The old unanswered questionings.

BY THE ANNIO.

(PASTORAL.)

HERE where shallows ripple by,
And the woody banks are high,
Every little wind that frets
Waves the scent of violets ;
Here the greening beech has made
Such a palace of cool shade,
You and I would rather sit
Silent in the shade of it,
Seeking questions and replies
Only through each other's eyes.
Sweet, than climb the thorny ways
Up their barren hills of praise.
In the gloom of yonder glen
Hides the crimson cyclamen,
And the tall narcissus still
Lingers near the reedy rill,
In the ooze the rushes grow
Pipes for merry lips to blow;

Here the songs that we shall sing
Shall be all of love or spring ;
Here the emerald dragon-fly
Flits and stays and passes by,
While the bird that overhead
Mocked our song, grows unafraid,
Splashing till his breast be cool
At the margin of the pool.
In my hand the hand I hold
Lies more daintily than gold ;
On your lips is all the praise
I would barter for my lays,
In your eyes I look to see
Witness of my sovereignty.
They that long for high estate
Turn to look for love too late,
Climbing on at last they find
Love has long been left behind ;
Sweet, we do not envy these
In our riverland of trees.

Seldom feet of mortals pass
Here along the dewy grass ;

Only in the loneliest spot,
Where the woodman enters not,
Spirits of these groves and springs
Make their nightly wanderings.
Never now they walk at day
Since the Satyrs fled away,
Only when the fireflies gleam
Up the winding wooded stream,
You may hear low silver tones,
Like the ripple on the stones,
Asking some familiar star
Where their olden lovers are.
Listen, listen, up above
All the branches sing of love !
When the world is tired of May,
When the springtide fades away,
When the clouds draw over head,
And the moon of love is dead,
When the joy is no more new,
Seek we other work to do !
Only while the heart is young
Let no other song be sung !

BY THE CRUCIFIX.

HE tells his story with his young sad eyes,
   The rags are drooping from his sunburnt breast,
   He had sat down a little while to rest,
Far off the country of his longing lies ;

He sits there looking at his bare bruised feet
   And sees the rich man and the priest pass by,
   There where the crucifix is planted high
On the grass bank outside the village street.

Beside him lies his little flageolet—
   The children danced that morning when he played,
   Laughed loud to hear the music that he made ;—
Now the day closes and he wanders yet.

Oh, if some one of all the folk who pass,
   Would turn and speak one word and hear him
     though,
   And help !   It were so small a thing to do ;
And all they see him lying in the grass.

So the day ended, and the evening sun
    Cast the long shadows down ; he turned and saw
    The crucifix blood-red, and in mute awe,
He crossed himself, and shuddered, and went on.

And then, it seemed that the pale form above
    Moved slowly, lifting up the thorn-crowned head,
    And the drooped eyelids opened, and he said,
" Oh, ye who make profession of your love,

" With voices echoing a hollow cry,
    My name is ever on your lips, and yet
    I wander wearily and ye forget,
I am as nothing to you passers by,

" I had no heed of any shame or loss,
    And will ye leave me tired and homeless still
    Oh, call my name by any name ye will,
But leave me not for ever on my cross !"

"UNE HEURE VIENDRA QUI TOUT PAIERA."

IT was a tomb in Flanders, old and grey,
    A knight in armour, lying dead, unknown
    Among the long-forgotten, yet the stone
Cried out for vengeance where the dead man lay ;

No name was chiselled at his side to say
    What wrongs his spirit thirsted to atone,
    Only the armour with green moss o'ergrown,
And those grim words no years had worn away.

It may be haply in the songs of old
    His deeds were wonders to sweet music set,
    His name the thunder of a battle call,
Among the things forgotten and untold ;
    His only record is the dead man's threat—
    " An hour will come that shall atone for all !"

IN THE ALPS.

IT is spring by now in the world, but here
The doom of winter on all the year ;
A little brown bird flits to and fro,
Watching perhaps for a rift of blue
Where the mists divide and the sky looks through,
Or a crocus-bell in the half-thawed snow.

Little brown bird, have you no nest here
When winds blow cold in the long starlight ?
Never a tree, and the fields so white—
And are you ever a wayfarer ?
It is spring by now in the vales below,
And why do you stay in the world of snow ?

IN NOTRE DAME DE . . . .

THERE were two had died one day
So they told me by the way ;
" One, ah well, poor soul," they said,
" Better off that he is dead,
Such a poor man !—but the other
He was our good prefect's brother ;
Rich !   And surely of great worth ;—"
Both at one now—earth and earth !—
" Half the town is deep in prayer ;
Round him at our Lady's there ;
But the poor man's funeral
Is in the church outside the wall ;
Aye, our Lady's nave is wide,
Would you lay them side by side ?"
So I followed both these dead ;—
Where the poor man's pall was spread,
Boarded in his box of deal,
There were only six to kneel,

And a priest that hurried through
Such quick office as would do.
Requiem æternam dona ei, Domine,
  Et lux perpetua luceat ei.

Oh, but here how good to see
The great sable canopy !
All the columns shrouded o'er,
The rich curtains at the door,
And the purple velvet pall,
And the high catafalque o'er all,
Where a hundred tapers glow
On the same pale face of death below.—
All the good town's folk are there,
Some to weep and some to stare ;
Little recks *he* how ye weep,
Very sound he lies asleep ;
Little recks *he* how ye pray,
For his ears are sealed alway !
  Many a monk to thumb his beads,
Chant his canticles and creeds ;
Aye and here with quivering lips
O'er his meagre finger-tips

Prays the priest, and all the while
Drones the deep organ thrill ; and then
Along the gloomy curtained aisle,
Swells the full chant again ;
Requiem æternam dona ei, Domine,
Et lux perpetua luceat ei.

Now beyond the city wall
Winds his pomp of funeral;
Feebly do those tapers flare
In the sunshine's summer glare,
Loud above their chanting swells
The horror of the tolling bells,
Tapers burn where light is needed
For the living, not the dead !
Aye, and if your chants be heeded,
For the living be they said !
Where were all this folk who pray
When the poor man passed this way ?

Long ago the spirit fled,
All of him that was of worth,
In his sojourning on earth ;
Wherefore o'er a body dead,
Need long litanies be said ?

Shall the jewelled cross he presses
In those bony hands of his,
Aught avail, when death caresses
With his equal mouldering kiss?
Shall the rosary they ~~twined~~ *tied*
Round and round his stiffened wrists,
Hold his body sanctified
From the worms, the socialists?
   Gaudea sempiterna possideat!

So the two that died one day
Travelled down the selfsame way,
One in simple coffin board
Painted cross along it scored,
One with all his high estate
Graven on the silver plate,
All the pomp that he could save
To adorn him in the grave,
Lily wreaths of eucharis
To cover those poor bones of his,
From the graveyard's mouldy sod,—
But the poor man's soul and this
   Went the same way up to God!
In Paradisum deducant te angeli,
  Æternam habeas requiem!

By the sable shrouded door,

Of our Lady's church once more !

Softly came low music floating from above,

    And a voice seemed to breathe its cadence

      through ;

" Peace, peace !   Lo this we did it of our love,

    There was so little we could do !"

Requiem æternam dona iis, Domine,

    Et lux æterna luceat iis.

TWO SONNETS.

I.—ACTEA.

WHEN the last bitterness was past, she bore
   Her singing Cæsar to the Garden Hill,
Her fallen pitiful dead emperor.
She lifted up the beggar's cloak he wore
   —The one thing living that he would not kill—
And on those lips of his that sang no more,
   That world-loathed head which she found lovely
     still,
   Her cold lips closed, in death she had her will.

Oh wreck of the lost human soul left free
   To gorge the beast thy mask of manhood
     screened !
   Because one living thing, albeit a slave,
   Shed those hot tears on thy dishonoured
     grave,
Although thy curse be as the shoreless sea,
   Because she loved, thou art not wholly fiend.

II.—IMPERATOR AUGUSTUS.

Is this the man by whose decree abide
    The lives of countless nations, with the trace
    Of fresh tears wet upon the hard cold face ?
—He wept, because a little child had died.

They set a marble image by his side,
    A sculptured Eros, ready for the chase ;
    It wore the dead boy's features, and the grace
Of pretty ways that were the old man's pride.

And so he smiled, grown softer now, and tired
    Of too much empire, and it seemed a joy
Fondly to stroke and pet the curly head,
The smooth round limbs so strangely like the dead,
    To kiss the white lips of his marble boy
And call by name his little heart's-desired.

AT LANUVIUM.

" Festo quid potius die
Neptuni faciam."
Horace, *Odes*, iii. 28.

Spring grew to perfect summer in one day,
    And we lay there among the vines, to gaze
Where Circe's isle floats purple, far away
    Above the golden haze ;

And on our ears there seemed to rise and fall
    The burden of an old world song we knew,
That sang, " To-day is Neptune's festival,
    And we, what shall we do ?"

Go down brown-armed Campagna maid of mine,
    And bring again the earthen jar that lies
With three years' dust above the mellow wine ;
    And while the swift day dies.

You first shall sing a song of waters blue,
    Paphos and Cnidos in the summer seas,
And one who guides her swan-drawn chariot through
    The white-shored Cyclades ;

And I will take the second turn of song,
  Of floating tresses in the foam and surge
Where Nereid maids about the sea-god throng ;
  And night shall have her dirge.

A ROMAN MIRROR.

THEY found it in her hollow marble bed,
  There where the numberless dead cities sleep,
  They found it lying where the spade struck deep,
A broken mirror by a maiden dead.

These things—the beads she wore about her throat
  Alternate blue and amber all untied,
  A lamp to light her way, and on one side
The toll-men pay to that strange ferry-boat.

No trace to-day of what in her was fair!
  Only the record of long years grown green
  Upon the mirror's lustreless dead sheen,
Grown dim at last, when all else withered there.

Dead, broken, lustreless! It keeps for me
  One picture of that immemorial land,
  For oft as I have held thee in my hand
The dull bronze brightens, and I dream to see

A fair face gazing in thee wondering wise,
    And o'er one marble shoulder all the while
    Strange lips that whisper till her own lips smile,
And all the mirror laughs about her eyes.

It was well thought to set thee there, so she
    Might smooth the windy ripples of her hair
    And knot their tangled waywardness, or ere
She stood before the queen Persephone.

And still it may be where the dead folk rest
    She holds a shadowy mirror to her eyes,
    And looks upon the changelessness and sighs,
And sets the dead land lilies in her breast.

THE SONG OF THE DEAD CHILD.

FLORENCE, '81.

By the light of their waxen tapers, I saw not ever a
tear,
For the child in its bridal garment, the little dead
child on the bier.

Some child of the poor ;—I wonder, was it glad that
the years were done,
This flower that fell in spring tide, and had hardly
looked on the sun ?

They have decked her in burial raiment, they have
twined a wreath for her hair ;
Ah child, you had never in life such delicate dress to
wear !

And the man in the pilgrim's habit has covered the
marble head,
And carried it out for ever to the sleeping place of
the dead.

Rest, little one, have no fear, you will hardly turn in
    your sleep,
Though the moon and the stars are clouded, and the
    grave they have made be deep !

But an hour before the dawning there will come one
    down on the night,
With the wings and the brows of an angel, in wonder-
    robes of white.

He will smile in your eyes of wonder, he will take
    your hand in his hand,
And gather you up in his arms and pass from the
    sleeping land.

Then after a while, at morning, you will come to the
    lands that lie
On the other side of the sunrise between the cloud
    and the sky,

And here is the place of resting with the wings of
    your angel furled,
For the feet that are tired with travel in the dusty
    ways of the world.

And here is the children's meeting, the length of a
    summer's day,
You will gather you crowns of roses, in the deep
    meadow lands at play.

While up through the clouds dividing, like a sweet
    bewildering dream,
You will watch the wings of the angels drift by in an
    endless stream ;

Such marvellous robes are o'er them, and whiter are
    some than snows,
And some like the April blossom, and some like the
    pale primrose.

For these are the hues of day-dawn that you saw
    from the world of old,
And the first light over the mountains was shed from
    their crowns of gold ;

And many go by with weeping, for ever, the long
    night through,
The tears of the sorrowing angels fall over the earth
    in dew ;

Till your eyes grow weary of wonder as you sit in the
    long cool grass,
And many will bend and kiss you of the wonderful
    forms that pass ;

With your head on the breast of the angel there will
    steal down over your eyes
The sleep of the long forgetting, and the dream
    where memory dies,

As the flowers are washed in the night-time, when
    the dew drops down from above,
You will reck no more of the winter, and hunger, and
    want of love.

Then at last it will seem like even when you waken,
    and hand in hand
You will pass with your angels guiding, to the
    utmost verge of the land ;

And I think you will hear far voices growing musical
    there, and loud,
As you pass, with an unfelt swiftness, from luminous
    cloud to cloud ;

Till the light shall turn to a glory, that seemed but
    a lone faint star,
That will be the gate of Heaven, where the souls of
    the children are.

NIGHT AT AVIGNON.

No cloud between the myriad stars and me,—
   Soft music moving o'er a sleeping land
Of winds that fret about the cypress tree,
   And Rhone's swift rapids rippling past the sand.
Arch over arch, and tower on battled wall,
   Against the violet deepness of the skies ;—
And one grey spire set high above them all,
   Where round the hill the moon begins to rise.
An hour's knell rings softly out once more
   From unseen cloisters, where the misty bridge
Fades in the distance of the further shore,
And nearer spires repeat it o'er and o'er ;
   One great blue star peers through the seaward
      ridge ;
A hollow footfall up the echoing street
   Goes wandering out to silence, and the breeze
Drops faint and fainter, here beneath my feet
   The grass is all with violets overstrewn ;
Oh listen, listen ; in yon garden trees

Do you not hear the lute that lovers use!
One sets the discord of its strings atune ;—
And in the dreamland of the risen moon
    They sing some olden love-song of Vaucluse.

"WHERE THE RHONE GOES DOWN TO THE SEA."

A SWEET still night of the vintage time,
  Where the Rhone goes down to the sea ;
The distant sound of a midnight chime
  Comes over the wave to me.
Only the hills and the stars o'erhead
  Bring back dreams of the days long dead,
While the Rhone goes down to the sea.

The years are long, and the world is wide,
And we all went down to the sea ;
  The ripples splash as we onward glide,
And I dream they are here with me—
  All lost friends whom we all loved so,
In the old mad life of long ago,
  Who all went down to the sea.

So we passed in the golden days
  With the summer down to the sea.

They wander still over weary ways,
  And come not again to me.
I am here alone with the night wind's sigh,
  The fading stars, and a dream gone by,
And the Rhone going down to the sea.

AT TIBER MOUTH.

THE low plains stretch to the west with a glimmer
  of rustling weeds,
Where the waves of a golden river wind home by
  the marshy meads ;
And the fresh wind born of the sea grows faint
  with a sickly breath,
As it stays in the fretting rushes and blows on the
  dews of death.
We came to the silent city, in the glare of the
  noontide heat,
When the sound of a whisper rang through the
  length of the lonely street ;
No tree in the clefted ruin, no echo of song nor
  sound,
But the dust of a world forgotten lay under the
  barren ground.
There are shrines under these green hillocks to the
  beautiful gods that sleep,
Where they prayed in the stormy season for lives
  gone out on the deep ;

And here in the grave street sculptured, old record
  of loves and tears,

By the dust of the nameless slave, forgotten a
  thousand years.

Not ever again at even shall ship sail in on the
  breeze,

Where the hulls of their gilded galleys came home
  from a hundred seas,

For the marsh plants grow in her haven, the marsh
  birds breed in her bay,

And a mile to the shoreless westward the water has
  passed away.

But the sea-folk gathering rushes come up from the
  windy shore,

So the song that the years have silenced grows
  musical there once more ;

And now and again unburied, like some still voice
  from the dead,

They light on the fallen shoulder and the lines of a
  marble head.

But we went from the sorrowful city and wandered
  away at will,

And thought of the breathing marble and the words
  that are music still.

G 2

How full were their lives that laboured, in their
    fetterless strength and far

From the ways that our feet have chosen as the
    sunlight is from the star,

They clung to the chance and promise that once
    while the years are free

Look over our life's horizon as the sun looks over
    the sea,

But we wait for a day that dawns not, and cry for
    unclouded skies,

And while we are deep in dreaming the light that
    was o'er us dies ;

We know not what of the present we shall stretch
    out our hand to save

Who sing of the life we long for, and not of the life
    we have ;

And yet if the chance were with us to gather the
    days misspent,

Should we change the old resting-places, the wan-
    dering ways we went ?

They were strong, but the years are stronger ; they
    are grown but a name that thrills,

And the wreck of their marble glory lies ghost-like
    over their hills.

So a shadow fell o'er our dreaming for the weary
    heart of the past,
For the seed that the years have scattered, to reap
    so little at last.
And we went to the sea-shore forest, through a long
    colonnade of pines,
Where the skies peep in and the sea, with a flitting
    of silver lines.
And we came on an open place in the green deep
    heart of the wood
Where I think in the years forgotten an altar of
    Faunus stood ;
From a spring in the long dark grasses two rivulets
    rise and run
By the length of their sandy borders where the snake
    lies coiled in the sun.
And the stars of the white narcissus lie over the grass
    like snow,
And beyond in the shadowy places the crimson
    cyclamens grow ;
Far up from their wave home yonder the sea-winds
    murmuring pass,
The branches quiver and creak and the lizard starts
    in the grass.

And we lay in the untrod moss and pillowed our
    cheeks with flowers,
While the sun went over our heads, and we took
    no count of the hours ;
From the end of the waving branches and under the
    cloudless blue,
Like sunbeams chained for a banner, the thread-like
    gossamers flew.
And the joy of the woods came o'er us, and we felt
    that our world was young
With the gladness of years unspent and the sorrow
    of life unsung.
So we passed with a sound of singing along to the
    seaward way,
Where the sails of the fishermen folk came homeward
    over the bay;
For a cloud grew over the forest and darkened the
    sea-god's shrine,
And the hills of the silent city were only a ruby
    line.
But the sun stood still on the waves as we passed
    from the fading shores,
And shone on our boat's red bulwarks and the golden
    blades of the oars,

And it scemed as we steered for the sunset that we
  passed through a twilight sea,
From the gloom of a world forgotten to the light of
  a world to be.

GARIBALDI IN ROME.

JUNE 29-30, 1849.

ST. PETER'S eve, from dim Janiculum
  The battle's thunder drowned the bells that tolled,
The great guns flashed, but that night as of old
  We kept St. Peter's vigil, and the dome
Blazed with its myriad little lamps of gold,
And all the river ran with yellow foam,
  While on the torchlit Capitol unrolled
The banner blew of our Republic, Rome,

Then silence fell with treacherous midnight,—
  An hour ere dawn we heard a wild alarm,
  The blast of bugles, the swift call to arm,
We sang his war hymn and fell in to fight ;
  Then as dawn gathered on the Esquiline
  Our grand old lion gave the battle sign.

'ΕΡΑΝ ΤΩΝ 'ΑΔΥΝΑΤΩΝ.

now I know we shall not any more,
  As we have done in these last golden days,
  Go hand in hand along life's pleasant ways,
Walk heart with heart together as before.

It seems we cannot choose but wear the chain
  Fate winds about our little lives. Ah sweet,
  What wall is set between us that your feet
Must wander alway where I gaze in vain!

Could we have climbed together! How these bars
  Had melted in the fire of love ; the road
  Had known our footsteps where the wise men trod,
And our sure ways had ended with the stars!

We had atoned for passion !—passed above
  All fleeting shadows of the world's desire,
  Made pure our spirits at a holier fire,
And in the lap of morning laid our love.

One law I knew, one right, one starward way,
    One hope to make our lives divine, one love
    In this one life, one star of truth above,
And one great desert where the rest go stray.

Life had no more to give, if that we two
    Had let the world go gladly, grasp and reach
    Strained ever upward, leaning each on each,
Had seen one star-ray of the pure and true.

Had we but climbed together! Oh my light,
    My star, my moon, and art thou clouded o'er?
    And we that were together, evermore
Must stand apart and stare across the night!

One life it seems must take its tale of days,
    And as it may make service of its own,
    But ah! the infinite help of love!—alone
The heart grows faint and weary of dispraise.

I shall be braver on the way I go,
    Hearing that voice forever, for whose sake,
    What burthen had I not bowed down to take,
What shame or peril, had it helped you so!

This must content me, to have loved, who lose
   In this hard world where little loves live on,
   No man will love you as I might have done,
Sweet heart, too holy for the world to choose !

Therefore be strong, remembering love's past,
   Climb on for ever in the steep old way
   That haply so a moment's space we may
Meet on the verge of changes at the last.

That at the end of all these journeyings,
   Crossing the borderland of time and space
   We two may stand together face to face,
Whose hearts were set upon abiding things,
And through the cloud-veil of Eternity
   Our eyes may meet at last in the full light, and see.

TRANSLATIONS.

From the Italian of Stecchetti.

I.

WHEN the sere leaves fall and you come one day
  To find me under the graveyard stone,
It will be in a corner hidden away,
  With beds of flowers about it grown.

Then gather and wreathe in your golden hair
The flowers that grow from my heart laid there.

They will be love's message I might not bring,
And the rest of the songs that I meant to sing.

II.

Floweret born in the hedge-row shade
  Set out of sight alone,
Love like thee must hide his head
Love like thee must live unknown.

No smile of the sun, and thou wilt die,
  Thorns round thee and above,
No smile of hope, and love will die,
  And none take heed.—Poor love !   Poor love !

————

From the German of Heine.

I.

How the mirrored moonbeams quiver
  On the waters' fall and rise,
Yet the moon serene as ever
  Wanders through the quiet skies.

Like the mirrored moonlight's fretting
  Are the dreams I have of you,
For my heart will beat, forgetting
  You are ever calm and true.

II.

So fair and pure and holy,
  So flowerlike thou art,
And while I gaze the shadow
  Grows deeper on my heart ;

I want my hands to rest on
   That head of thine in prayer,
That God will keep thee alway
   So holy pure and fair.

III.

The leaves are falling, falling,
   The yellow treetops wave,
Ah, all delight and beauty
   Is drawing to the grave.

About the wood's crest flicker
   The wan sun's laggard rays,
They are the parting kisses
   Of fleeting summer days.

Mescems I should be shedding
   The heart's-tears from my eyes,
The day will keep recalling
   The time of our good-byes.

I knew that you were dying
   And I must pass away,
Oh I was the waning summer,
   And you were the wood's decay.

IV.

From my tears that have fallen a flower
   Is springing along the vale,
And the sighs I have sighed endower
   The song of a nightingale.

And, child, if you'll be my lover,
   The flowers shall all be yours,
And the bird with its song shall hover
   For ever before your doors.

AVE ATQUE VALE.

I.

AND he is gone !—like strain of viols parted—
　　Back to the infinite from whence he came,
And we sit here, bereft and weary hearted,
　　New songs may wake, but not again the same.

Our hearts were lutes, whereon he used to play,
　　Now evermore is silence on that key,
And thought grows chilly like a sunless day
　　That greys the ripple on the haggard sea.

Those lips were cold that lingering we kissed,
　　There came no pressure from the old true hand,
A little while and through the twilight mist
　　We scarce shall trace his footprints in the sand.

II.

THIS was the end love made,—the hard-drawn
   breath,
The last long sigh that ever man sighs here ;
And then for us, the great unanswered fear,
Will love live on,—the other side of death ?

Only a year, and I had hoped to spend
A life of pleasant communing, to be
A kindred spirit holding fast to thee,
We never thought that love had such an end.

This was the end love made, for our delight,
For one sweet year he cannot take away ;—
Those tapers burning in the dim half-light,
Those kneeling women with a cross that pray,
And there, beneath green leaves and lilies white,
Beyond the reach of love, our loved one lay.

III.

HE had the poet's eyes,
    —Sing to him sleeping,—
Sweet grace of low replies,
    —Why are we weeping ?

He had the gentle ways,
    —Fair dreams befall him !—
Beauty through all his days,
    —Then why recall him ?—

That which in him was fair
    Still shall be ours :
Yet, yet my heart lies there
    Under the flowers.

"IF ANY ONE RETURN."

I WOULD we had carried him far away
   To the light of this south sun land,
Where the hills lean down to some red-rocked bay
And the sea's blue breaks into snow-white spray
   As the wave dies out on the sand.

Not there, not there, where the winds deface!
   Where the storm and the cloud race by!
But far away in this flowerful place
Where endless summers retouch, retrace,
   What flowers find heart to die.

And if ever the souls of the loved, set free,
   Come back to the souls that stay,
I could dream he would sit for a while with me,
Where I sit by this wonderful tideless sea,
   And look to the red-rocked bay,

By the high cliff's edge where the wild weeds twine,
   And he would not speak or move,
But his eyes would gaze from his soul at mine,—
My eyes that would answer without one sign,
   And that were enough for love.

And I think I should feel as the sun went round
   That he was not there any more,
But dews were wet on the grass-grown mound
On the bed of my love lying underground,
   And evening pale on the shore.

HIC JACET.

Did you play here, child,
　　The whole spring through,
And smiled and smiled
　　And never knew?—
Where the shade is cool
　　And the grass grows deep,
One that was beautiful
　　Lies in his sleep.

Ah no, child, never
　　Will he arise ;
The sleep was for ever
　　That closed his eyes.
And his bed is strewn
　　Deep underground,
He was tired so soon,
　　And now sleeps sound.

When the first birds sing
   We can hear them, dear,
And in early spring
   There are snowdrops here ;
For the flowers love him
   That lies below,
And ever above him
   The daisies grow.

" Shall we look down deep
   Where he hides away ?
Shall we find him asleep ?"
   Yes, child, some day.
But his palace gate
   Is so hard to see,
We two must wait
   For the angel's key.

"WHEN I AM DEAD."

WHEN I am dead, my spirit
　　Shall wander far and free
Through realms the dead inherit
　　Of earth, and sky, and sea ;
Through morning dawn and gloaming,
　　By midnight moons at will,
By shores where the waves are foaming,
　　By seas where the waves are still.
I, following late behind you,
　　In wingless sleepless flight,
Will wander till I find you,
　　In sunshine or twilight ;
With silent kiss for greeting
　　On lips, and eyes, and head,
In that strange after-meeting
　　Shall love be perfected.
We shall lie in summer breezes,
　　And pass where whirlwinds go,
And the Northern blast that freezes
　　Shall bear us with the snow.

We shall stand above the thunder,
　　And watch the lightnings hurled
At the misty mountains under,
　　Of the dim forsaken world,
We shall find our footsteps' traces,
　　And passing hand in hand
By old familiar places,
　　We shall laugh, and understand.

ST. CATHARINE OF EGYPT.

THERE was a king's one daughter long ago,
In ways of summer, where the swallows go,
For whom no prince was found in any land
Fair lived and clean to wed so white a hand ;
Who lying wakeful on a moonless night
Saw the dim ways grow tremulous with light,
As the sun's dawning glory, and was aware
Of a pale woman standing shrouded there,
With hands locked in another's hands, whose eyes
Shone like the starriest wonder of the skies.

And the pale woman bending o'er her bed
Unveiled the pity in her eyes, and said,
" Lo this is he whose blameless days were sweet,
If thou could'st love him, and thy love was meet."
And yet he turned those lustrous brows away,
And a sad voice seemed evermore to say
Across the stillness of a world that slept,
" Not mine, not mine,"—so all night through she wept
And never heard the singing nightingales.

Then awhile after when the cloudy sails
Of many a day had winged across the sky,
And she had gathered all the mystery
From a lone hermit in a desert wood,
He came once more in the night-time and stood
And set a bridal ring upon her hand
To be his lady in his father's land.
So in a little while her rumour grew
Till the rough Roman angered—her they slew
Being too sweet and wise for that rude time
That murdered pity and made love a crime.

And the wise men were glad when she was dead,
For they had failed of reason—she had said,
"When I come up into my kingdom there
And my Lord greets me, and I speak him fair,
Then will I take him by the hand with me
And lead him down, how far so e'er it be,
Until we find the old man, Socrates,
And the fair souls who followed, for all these
Will be together, and I will bid him take
Their hands in his and love them for my sake,
Because of old they brought me near his side."

It was the time of even when she died ;
And a fair choir of angels swept along
The dying afterglow, before their song
The gates were loosed and through the broken bars
They bore her skyward under the chill stars,
Westward—but once alighting as they flew.
In a deep meadow-land, with soft night-dew,
They washed the tender wounded throat, and kissed
The cords that bound her delicate soft wrist,
And at their kiss the fetters fell in twain
And the white robe grew faultless of one stain.
Then onward, ever onward, all night through,
Till lustreless the moon of morning grew
In the pale sky where one star lingered yet.

Some dark-browed fisher, as he cast his net
And woke a ripple on the waveless calm,
Looked up and heard the passing angels' psalm,
And through the ripple of the water-rings
He saw the gleam of rainbow-tinted wings
Drift o'er the glassing bosom of the sea.

There where the grave of innocence should be,
High up between the rock ridge and the sky,

Upon the holy summit Sinai,
Above the red sea's summer-tranced wave
They laid their burden in a marble grave.
And there her beauty flecteth not, decay
Can never steal her loveliness away,
But like a carven image evermore
Sleeps on now with her still hands folded o'er
The saint's white lily ever blossoming,—
All that was earthly of so fair a thing.

ATALANTA.

WAIT not along the shore, they will not come ;
The suns go down beyond the windy seas,
Those weary sails shall never wing them home
      O'er this white foam ;
      No voice from these
On any landward wind that dies among the trees.

Gone south, it may be, rudderless, astray,
Gone where the winds and ocean currents bore,
Out of all tracks along the sea's highway
      This many a day,
      To some far shore
Where never wild seas break, or any fierce winds
   roar.

For there are lands ye never recked of yet
Between the blue of stormless sea and sky,
Beyond where any suns of yours have set,
      Or these waves fret ;
      And loud winds die
In cloudless summertide, where those far islands lie.

They will not come! for on the coral shore
The good ship lies, by little waves caressed,
All stormy ways and wanderings are o'er,
    No more, no more!
    But long sweet rest,
In cool green meadow-lands, that lie along the West.

Or if beneath far fathom depths of waves
She lies heeled over by the slow tide's sweep,
Deep down where never any swift sea raves,
    Through ocean caves,
    A dreaming deep
Of softly gliding forms, a glimmering world of sleep.

Then have they passed beyond the outer gate
Through death to knowledge of all things, and so
From out the silence of their unkown fate
    They bid us wait,
    Who only know
That twixt their loves and ours the great seas ebb
    and flow.

THEORETIKOS.

A Thought of Darwin.

HE dwelt unblinded with eternal truth,
Through long communion perfected, not once
Did he misdeem the prelude for the song,
And looking onward, to his ample view
That long to-come when he should be no more
Outweighed the moment of his passing here.

And he was happy, and his peace was full,
Having outlived the struggle—not as those
Who take the world on faith, and rest content
With the old verdicts, question, wonder not,
But feeling trusting loving are at peace.

He sought and found one little germ of truth,
Made pure his spirit of all chance and change,
Held fast on things abiding, learned to stand
On ever loftier summits—till at last
His brow grew starry and his searching eyes
Blue with the mirrored distance, and he heard
The everlasting music, Time and space
Were part with every heart-beat, and almost

God seemed to whisper in his listening ear.
What need for him of all your wonder world ?
He made the wonder visible—enough
This little handful of the common clay
A seed to sow therein, and then to watch
The hidden forces quicken into life,
Till leaf by leaf some flower-star unfolds,
One flower of all the flowers, because the sun
Is in the skies, one sun of all the suns.
Search but the structure of one daisy's heart
Your lore has no such miracle as this !—
And look at all the infinite device,
The texture of the leaves of all the trees—
Is there not marvel here enough?   And yet
Ye crave new signs and wonders to convince
And wander lost upon your devious ways.
Ye will but gaze upon a part, and grow
In little wisdom overwise, therefore
Your partial grasp is barren to conceive
The thought Infinity, Time wilders yet
Because ye measure with your finite gauge,
And Motion maddens through your own unrest.

     He let the world go gladly, hand in hand
He walked with Reason, till thought strained away

And God grew nearer,—so he built his mind
A bridge to span from sun to sun of all
The starry systems ;—like a faint far dream
The changing pageant of men's lives unrolled,
And he stood by serenely,—but with him
The calm was struggle in a lordlier way,
Absorbed and dwelling with eternal truth,
Whose star o'ershone him ; till it seemed that life
And death were one, and from the throbbing brow
The craving died away,—and now he rests
With that fair choir from many times whose souls
Have earned the right of knowledge after death.

ROME.

I.—FROM THE HILL OF GARDENS.

THE outline of a shadowy city spread
Between the garden and the distant hill—
And o'er yon dome the flame-ring lingers still,
Set like the glory on an angel's head :
The light fades quivering into evening blue
Behind the pine-tops on Ianiculum ;
The swallow whispered to the swallow "come !"
And took the sunset on her wings, and flew.

One rift of cloud the wind caught up suspending
A ruby path between the earth and sky ;
Those shreds of gold are angel wings ascending
From where the sorrows of our singers lie ;
They have not found those wandering spirits yet,
But seek for ever in the red sunset.

Pass upward angel wings !   Seek not for these,
They sit not in the cypress-planted graves ;
Their spirits wander over moonlit waves,
And sing in all the singing of the seas ;

And by green places in the spring-tide showers,
And in the re-awakening of flowers.

Some pearl-lipped shell still dewy with sea foam
Bear back to whisper where their feet have trod ;
They are the earth's for evermore ; fly home !
And lay a daisy at the feet of God.

II.—IN THE COLISEUM.

NIGHT wanes ; I sit in the ruin alone ;
Beneath, the shadow of arches falls
From the dim outline of the broken walls ;
And the half-light steals o'er the age-worn stone
From a midway arch where the moon looks through
A silver shield in the deep, deep blue.

This is the hour of ghosts that rise ;—
Line on line of the noiseless dead—
The clouds above are their awning spread ;
Look into the shadow with moon-dazed eyes,
You will see the writhing of limbs in pain,
And the whole red tragedy over again.

The ghostly galleys ride out and meet,
The Cæsar sits in his golden chair,
His fingers toy with his women's hair,
The water is blood-red under his feet,—
Till the owl's long cry dies down with the night,   .
And one star waits for the dawning light.

III.—IN A CHURCH.

THIS was the first shrine lit for Queen Marie ;
　　And I will sit a little at her feet,
　　For winds without howl down the narrow street
And storm-clouds gather from the westward sea.

Sweet here to watch the peasant people pray,
　　While through the crimson shrouded-window falls
　　Low light of even, and the golden walls
Grow dim and dreamful at the end of day.

Till from these columns fades their marble sheen,
　　And lines grow soft and mystical,—these wraiths
　　That watch the service of the changing faiths,
To Mary mother from the Cyprian queen.

But aye for me this old-word colonnade
　　Seems open to blue summer skies once more,
　　These altars pass, and on the polished floor
I see the lines of chequered light and shade ;

I seem to see the dark-browed Lybian lean
    To cool the tortured burning of 'he lash,
    I see the fountains as they leap' and flash,
The rustling sway of cypress set between.

And now yon friar with the bare feet there,
    Is grown the haunting spirit of the place ;
    Ah ! brown-robed friar with the shaven face,
The saints are weary of thy mumbled prayer.

From matins' bell to the slow day's decline
    He sits and thumbs his endless round of beads,
    Draws out the dreary cadence of his creeds,
And nods assent to each familiar line.

But she the goddess whose white star is set,
    Whose fane was pillaged for this sombre shrine,
    Could she look down upon those lips of thine,
And hear thee mutter, would she still regret ?

There came a sound of singing on my ear,
    And slowly glided through the far-off door
    A glimmer of grey forms like ghosts, they bore
A dead man lying on his purple bier.

Some poor man's soul, so little candle smoke
   Went curling upwards by the uncased shroud,
   And then a sudden thunder-clap broke loud,
And drowned the droning of the priest who spoke.

So all the shuffling feet passed out again
   To lightnings flashing through the wet and wind,
   And while I lingered in the gate behind
The dead man travelled through the storm and rain.

SEA PICTURES—FRANCE.

I. SUNSET.

ONE autumn evening from the west-most steep
I watched the daylight passing o'er the deep ;—
Down from the setting sun the great waves rolled
Along its seaward path of molten gold,
All the dark ocean rocks like capes of brass
Gleamed where the foam had washed them, and the
    grass
Grew glorious with that light, and the long swell
Line after line that followed, rose and fell
And shattered into frosted gold, the sky
Arched splendour over splendour,—isles that lie
Of crimson cloudland in pale seas of blue
Red bars of flame with one star peeping through,
Silent for glory ; and the sea's monotone
Grew part with silence ;—the great world rolled on
And the sun watched along the waves, until
The glow died upwards on the western hill,
And the shade saddened over all the sea
Reaching away, starward away from me
Into the twilight and Eternity.

II. TWILIGHT.

LATE evening now, and overclouded skies
To-night we shall not see the young moon rise ;
The twilight deepens, and on either hand
The cliffs are lost in mystic shadowland.
Only low sound of breakers as they die¦
Pale shimmer of waters and a pale still sky
Where darkness gathers on the moving sea,
And yet the child laughs light of heart with me !

Still deeper now ;—one little brown-sailed bark
Glides past us seaward, drifting into dark,
The only light is on the white sea-foam
And the lamp by the crucifix : Come home !

III. STORM.

NiGHT grows on the heaving ocean
 With its ominous white foam flakes,
And the dizzy eternal motion
 Where the crest of the wave line breaks,
With surge and swirl on the shingle
 Blown on by the keen sea wind,
Surf waves that recoil and mingle
 With the hurrying surf behind.

Low over the sea line yonder
 The gathering cloud-ranks form,
With a gleam of the sunset under
 The fringe of the boding storm.
Along the dim cliffs hollows
 The voice of the water moans,
Where the wave as it follows follows
 Tears on at the yielding stones.

The last day gleam departed,
 Wild gusts of a storm blast came,
And out of the cloud gloom darted
 The flash of the lightning flame,

And the pale, pale sea grew haggard
  A moment under the flash,
And the line of the dark rocks staggered
  And reeled from the thunder-crash :

Long loudly sullenly pealing
  It died in the cliffs afar,—
And I saw that a woman was kneeling
  At the cross by the harbour bar.

A LAST WORD.

TIME now to close these pages, far away
　　And fainter the old hills of childhood fade,
　　The very graves where the young dreams are laid
Are hidden deep in autumn leaves to-day.

It may be they have brought thee nearer truth,
　　These hasting years, but fain wouldst thou have
　　　　stayed
　　In the old land where trust was unbetrayed,
And love was honest in the eyes of youth.

And now it's winter, and the moon of snow
　　Blind mists of doubt, and chill unfriendly rain,
But somewhere, sometime in the year, we know
　　It must be spring and flowertime again.
Do thou but keep, though winter days be long,
Thy young love loyal, and thy young faith strong.

PRINTED BY BALLANTYNE, HANSON AND CO
LONDON AND EDINBURGH